Slime~A~Rella

—A Reimagined Fairy Tale—
By: Kendra Alston

Illustrated by :
Prosenjit Roy

She is a queen. Her soul is royalty.
-Adrian Michael

When I think of a fairy godmother,
I think of someone who unexpectedly
arrives to solve your problems, make good things
happen, or to remind you of your worth.

For My Aunt Janet,
my real life **Fairy Godmother**

When I was a young girl, you knew how to create
something magical out of that huge afro of mine.
Your amazing braid creations made me feel
beautiful, confident, and royal.

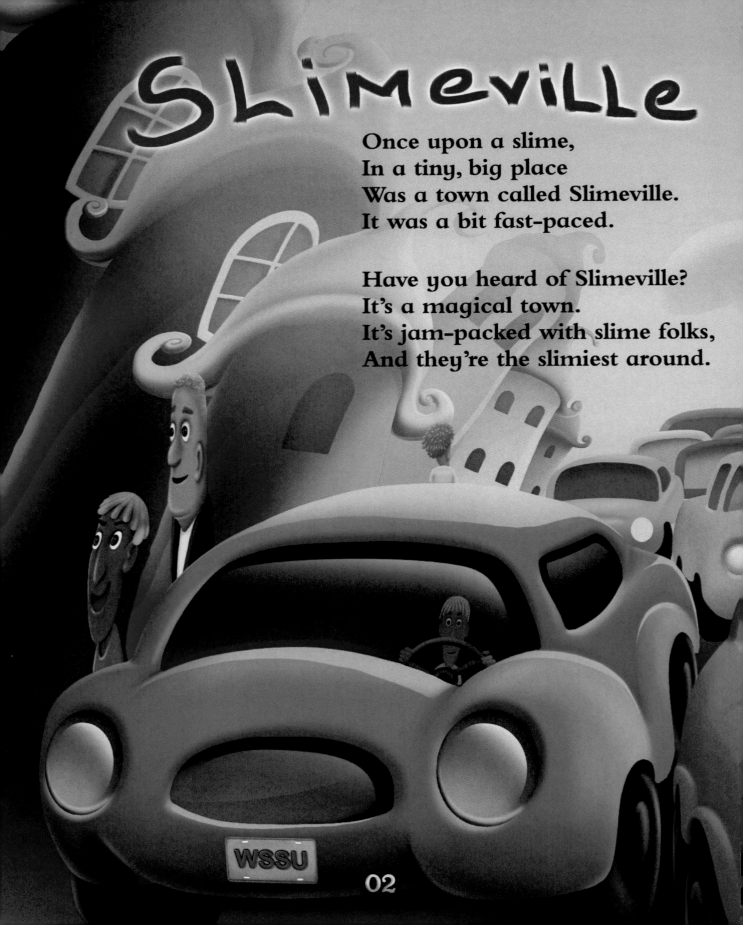

Slimeville

Once upon a slime,
In a tiny, big place
Was a town called Slimeville.
It was a bit fast-paced.

Have you heard of Slimeville?
It's a magical town.
It's jam-packed with slime folks,
And they're the slimiest around.

WSSU

Most slime folks were kind,
But some were not.
Some had very little,
And some had a lot.

They had one thing in common,
And it's really quite sublime:
The hair on their head
Was made mostly of *Slime*.

03

The folk of Slimeville
Took pride in their hair.
If not styled to perfection,
Slime folk would stare.

It was an unspoken rule,
And everyone knew
If you lived in Slimeville,
You had a stunning hairdo.

04

They wore slime puffs
And slime 'fros
And long, slimy locks,
Slime braids,
Crochets,
Slime fades and fauxhawks.

05

Barber shops and beauty stores
Lined the busy streets,
Further proof that in Slimeville,
Your hair was top priority.

Byron Blue Slime was Mayor,
Pelias Purple Slime was King,
Glenda Glow Slime was Queen,
And boy could she sing.

07

But the most handsome guy of all
(And his hair was supreme)
Was that magnetic Slime Prince—
But his friends call him Kareem.

08

All the girls in the land
Would love to date that fella,
But there was only ONE
who was worthy,
And her name?...

Slime~A~Rella

Karma
Hair Boutique

Slime-a-Rella was kind;
She was heaven-sent.
Her family owned a salon, but
She lived in the basement.

She had a stepmother
And two wicked sisters.
They made her clean up the salon
'Til she got slimy blisters.

12

They left globs here
And left globs there,
Slime hair on the mirrors,
Slime hair on the chairs.

13

Karma Hair Boutique

Her sisters were awful;
Their names were Stress and Heat.
They teased poor Slime-a-Rella
Because her hair wasn't neat.

"Clean our combs and our brushes.
Mop up that slime goo.
You look like a lion
From the Slimeville Zoo!

"You should really be ashamed
With that chubby, plain face.
Your hair looks like a mop;
It's all over the place.

14

"Who left that muck there?
Where's my green tea?
Scrub the hair goo from my sink
Immediately!"

15

Slime-a-Rella would work
From morning 'til night.
No matter what she did,
She never got it right.

Her days were full
Of cleaning sprees,
While Mom, Stress and Heat
Posted hairstyles on IG.

17

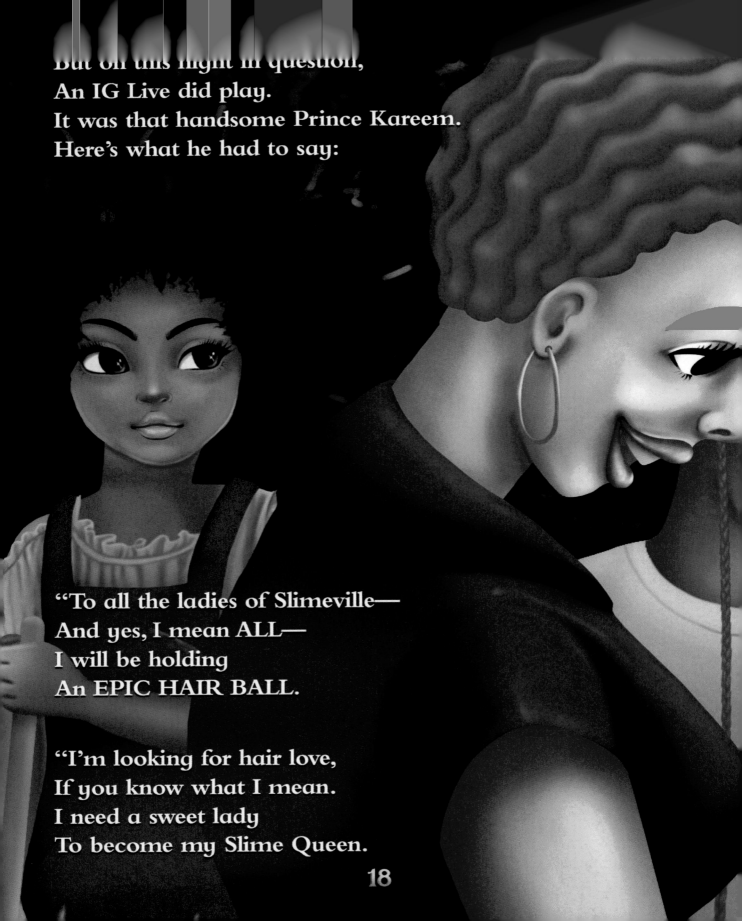

But on this night in question,
An IG Live did play.
It was that handsome Prince Kareem.
Here's what he had to say:

"To all the ladies of Slimeville—
And yes, I mean ALL—
I will be holding
An EPIC HAIR BALL.

"I'm looking for hair love,
If you know what I mean.
I need a sweet lady
To become my Slime Queen.

18

"So report to my palace
No later than five.
You better dress to impress—
I just may go LIVE."

19

The slime ladies in the salon
Were excited and thrilled
At the thought of becoming
The Hair Queen of Slimeville.

20

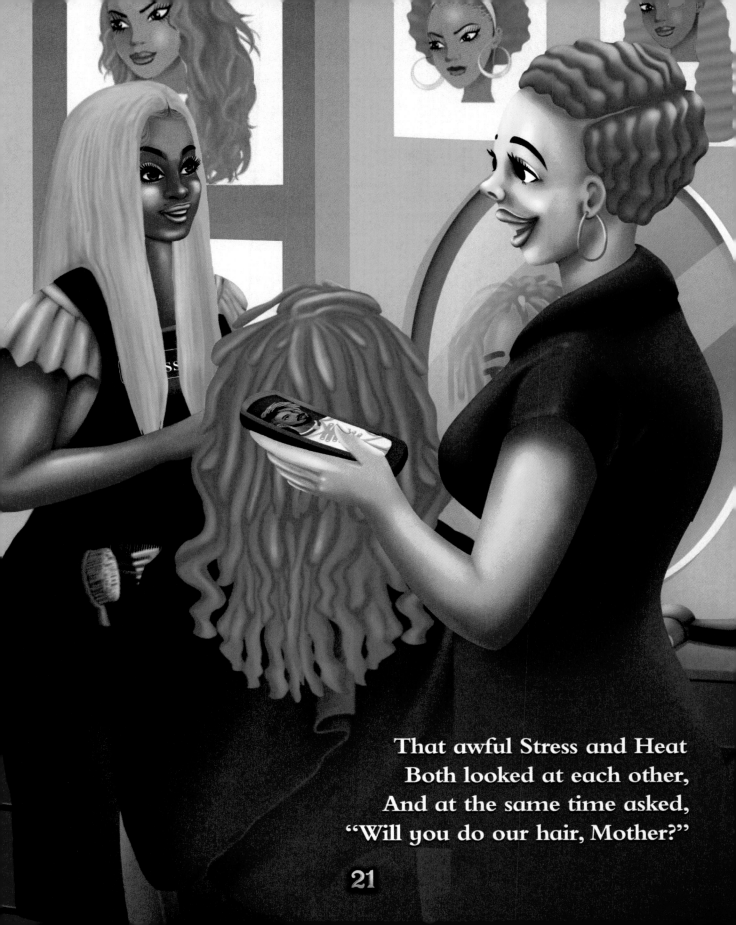

That awful Stress and Heat
Both looked at each other,
And at the same time asked,
"Will you do our hair, Mother?"

21

Slime-a-Rella was listening.
She wanted to go, too.
She wanted to see the prince
And behold his royal goo!

"Can I go too, Mom?"
Asked Slime-a-Rella, real shy.
"I'd love to meet the Prince,
Or at least say hi.

"It's been ten whole years
Since I have had my hair done,
And we could all go together.
Wouldn't that be fun?"

22

Mom looked at Stress and Heat.
"I'll help YOU TWO with YOUR styles,
But Slime-a-Rella, it's a no!
You won't embarrass me, lion child!"

They started laughing at 'Rella
As they pointed to her hair.
She really didn't know
How much more she could bear.

23

And when everyone left,
Slime-a-Rella did sigh.
She picked up a comb,
And then she started to cry.

"Oh, this just isn't fair!
They are all so unkind.
With a little comb and brush,
My hair would be fine."

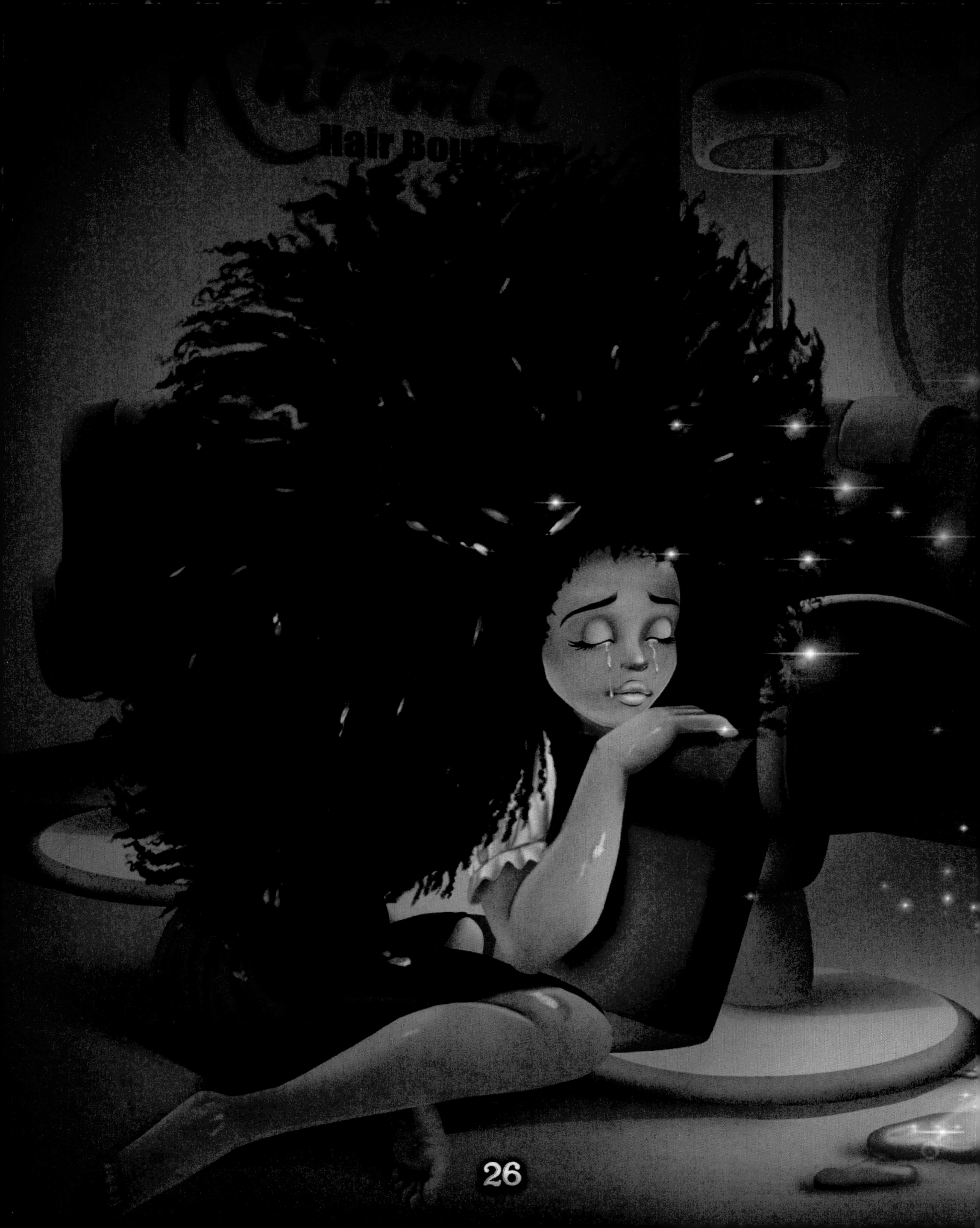
Hair

Whether by magic, or wishes,
Or dreams in the sky,
Perhaps hallucinations
Of beauty supplies,

'Rella wasn't sure what,
And she wasn't sure how,
But a glittery slime fairy
Just appeared somehow!

27

"I am Goo Glitter.
My glitter hair is my crown.
It feels and smells like cotton candy,
Like no other hair around.

"It sparkles in the morning
And glows in the night.
It attracts nature's beauty,
Like butterflies and sunlight.

"Your stepmom and sisters
Simply haven't been fair.
You're going to the ball
Because you belong there.

"Your hair is so healthy,
So shiny, it's true.
It's full of thick magic:
The very essence of you.

The fairy did something odd:
She cut a piece of Rella's hair,
Then took a magical cloth
And wiped tears off the chair.

"I'll save this for later,"
The Fairy Goo Mother said.
"Your tears and hair are important
For what lies ahead."

Slime-a-Rella was shocked,
Stunned and surprised.
Who was this lady
With glitter in her eyes?

"I'm here just to make
All your hair dreams come true.
Now answer me this:
Do you want me to help you?"

"Of course!" said Slime-a-Rella.
"Just tell me what to do!
I'll do anything for my prince.
Please help me, Fairy Goo!"

"Very well," said the fairy.
"I'll be here tomorrow night.
And we'll get you to that ball,
And you'll look a delight!"

The very next day,
As Slime-a-Rella waxed the tile,
Stress and Heat began creating
The perfect slime hairstyle.

They wanted a slime updo
That would really stand out.
Then Prince Kareem would choose THEM
Beyond a shadow of a doubt!

34

With their hair pinned up
And baby hair slicked in place,
Stress and Heat were now ready
To put a smile on Kareem's face.

Slime-a-Rella was watching
As she continued to wax and mop,
And when the clock struck four,
Stress and Heat left the shop.

35

And true to her word,
Like magic, like air,
Fairy Goo reappeared
And started parting Slime's
hair.

"Wait Fairy Goo,
Just wait, hold on.
My hair is a mess.
This will take way too long."

"Slime-a-Rella, please trust me,"
Said the glittery Fairy Goo.
"Let me use all my magic,
And watch what I do."

37

Integrity

Empathy

Self-worth

Resilience

Confidence

Humility

Balance

She took the tear-soaked cloth
And that piece of Slime's lock,
Took a spray can and sprayed it,
And put three seconds on the clock.

And like magic, 'Rella's hair
Had a beautiful, glittery glow.
She was almost ready
To go steal the show!

Her dress was amazing;
It sparkled and gleamed.
It matched her hair perfectly.
She was ready for Kareem.

And then from the sky,
Two hair pins came aglow—
The most beautiful glass pins
Patterned after rainbows.

Fairy Goo placed both hair pins
In the side of Slime's hair.
Fairy Goo said, "Don't lose these.
They are magical; they're rare.

39

"Now let me see.
I don't want to rush,
But watch what I do
With this spiky hair brush."

She zip-zapped the brush,
And it zipped and it tugged.
In three seconds flat,
It was a convertible VW Bug!

"With your hair and your dress
And your car oh so bright,
Go show off your hair,
But be gone by midnight!"

Slime-a-Rella took her car and
With very little hassle,
Made her way like a star
To Kareem's royal castle.

In no time at all,
The prince started to stare
At Slime-a-Rella in her dress
And all that beautiful slime hair.

"May I have this dance?"
Said the Prince of Slime.
"Of course, Your Highness.
But only for a short time."

They danced and they danced;
Prince Kareem was entranced.
None of the other slime girls
Even stood a chance.

And just as he was about
To touch her magical locks,
The clock struck midnight.
Oh, no! It was 12:00!

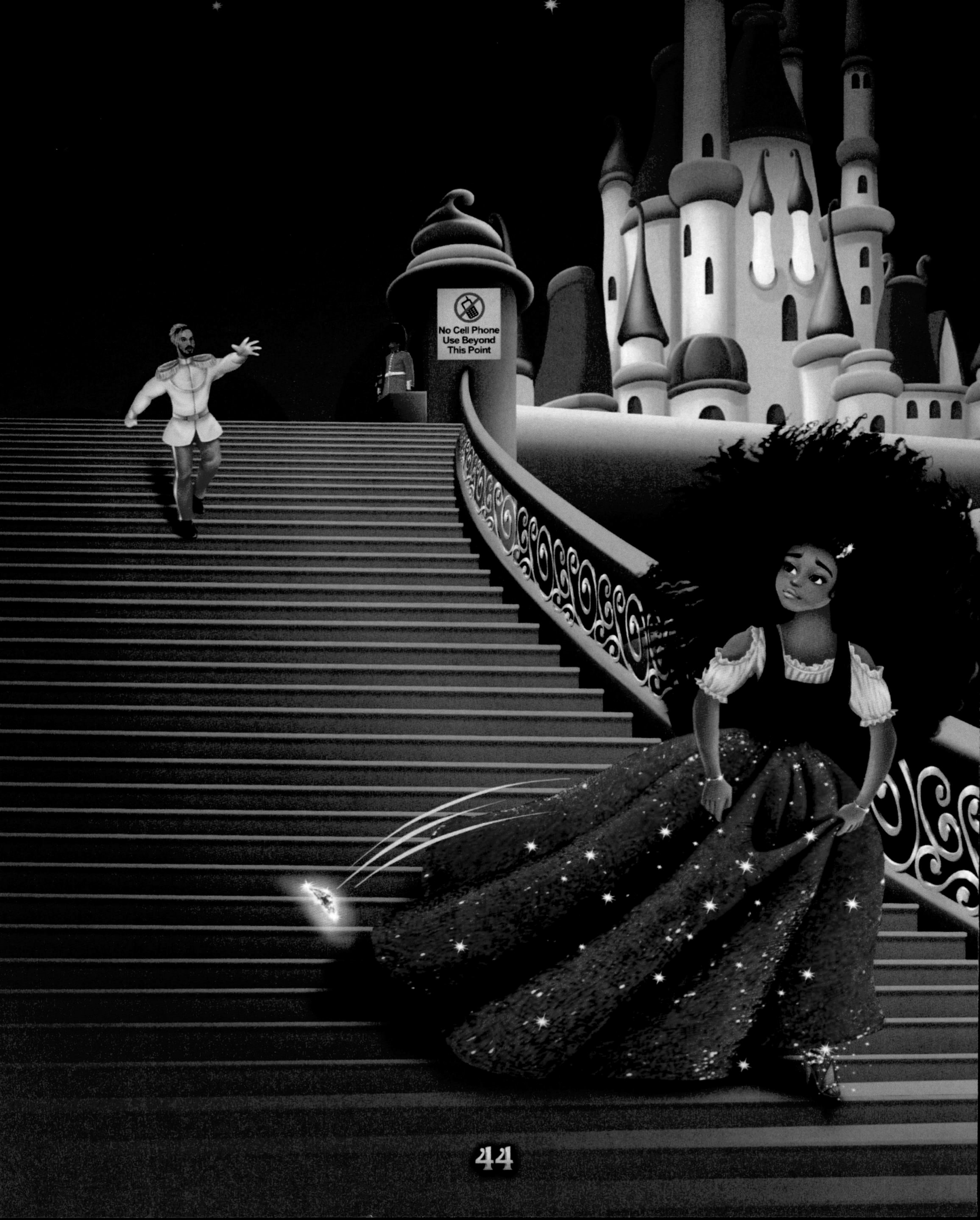
No Cell Phone
Use Beyond
This Point

So she turned and ran quickly
Down the platinum palace stairs
And never even noticed
The pin that fell from her hair.

Slime-a-Rella didn't realize
She was starting to look wack.
Her slime locks were quickly fading,
And her clothes were changing back.

45

Prince Kareem found the pin
And a lock of 'Rella's hair.
It was late in the night,
But he didn't care.

He was determined and
focused,
And in love, you see.
"I will find her tomorrow.
I'll post a photo on IG."

47

The prince stayed true to his word.
He was serious, no grins
In his post on IG,
Holding that magical hair pin.

"My party was lovely,
The best one in the world.
I found my true queen;
She had glorious slime curls.

"But she ran off too quickly
In the middle of the night,
And now it's my mission
To make things right.

"Whoever has the twin
To this beautiful pin
Will become my slime queen,
And my heart she will win."

The very next day,
Prince Kareem and his friends
Set out to find the girl
Who wore the rainbow-colored pin.

Natural hair, permed hair,
Colored hair, too.
Puffy hair, flat hair
And knots of Bantu.

Ladies came from all over
And brought next of kin,
But they couldn't find the match
To the beautiful hair pin.

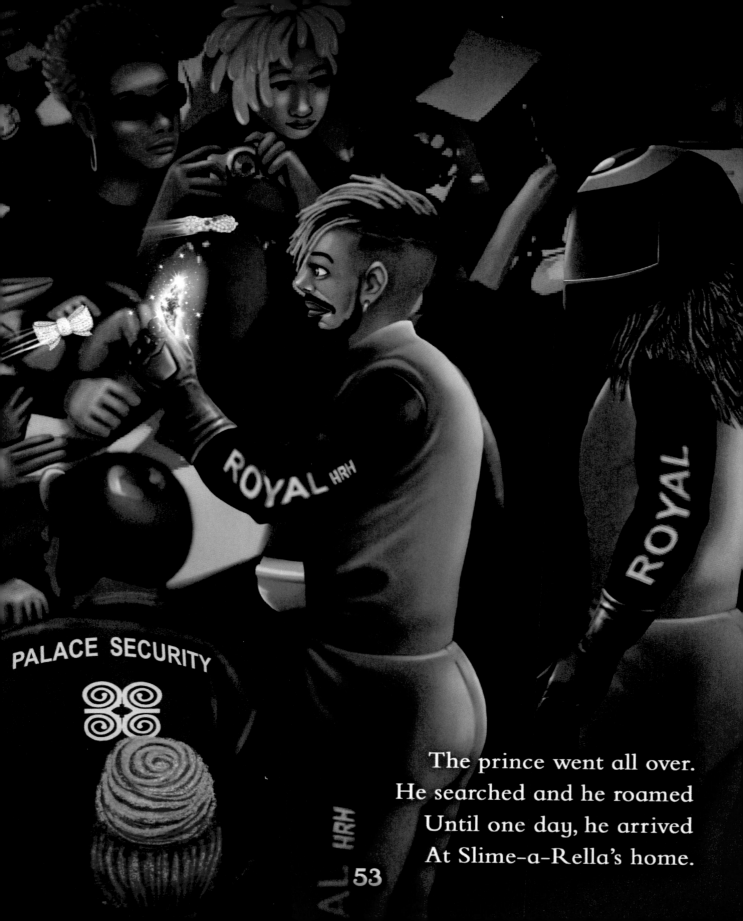

The prince went all over.
He searched and he roamed
Until one day, he arrived
At Slime-a-Rella's home.

53

Stress showed off her hair pins;
They were too old and rusty.
Heat showed off hers, too,
But hers smelled kind of musty.

Slime-a-Rella walked in.
"I have a hair pin, but it's bent."
"Don't be silly, slime girl.
Go back down to the basement."

55

But Slime-a-Rella was determined.
She knew what was fair.
She pulled that magical pin
From the depths of her hair.

Her sisters were shocked;
They felt really small.
They had no idea
She was at the Hair Ball.

"It was you, my Slime Queen!"
Kareem displayed a huge grin.
Then he reached in his jacket
And gave 'Rella the hair pin.

57

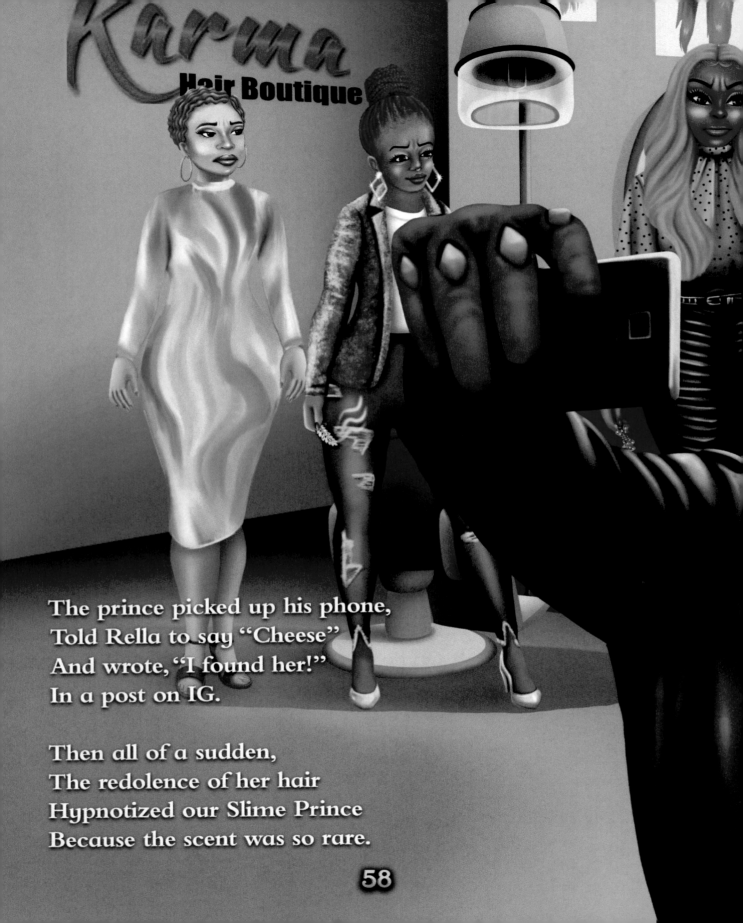

The prince picked up his phone,
Told Rella to say "Cheese"
And wrote, "I found her!"
In a post on IG.

Then all of a sudden,
The redolence of her hair
Hypnotized our Slime Prince
Because the scent was so rare.

Her hair smelled like peaches
And lavender root,
Aloe vera and pink sugar
And coconuts, too.

59

Kareem touched 'Rella's hair;
It had a cashmere feel.
How fitting for the girl
Who'd be the Hair Queen of Slimeville!

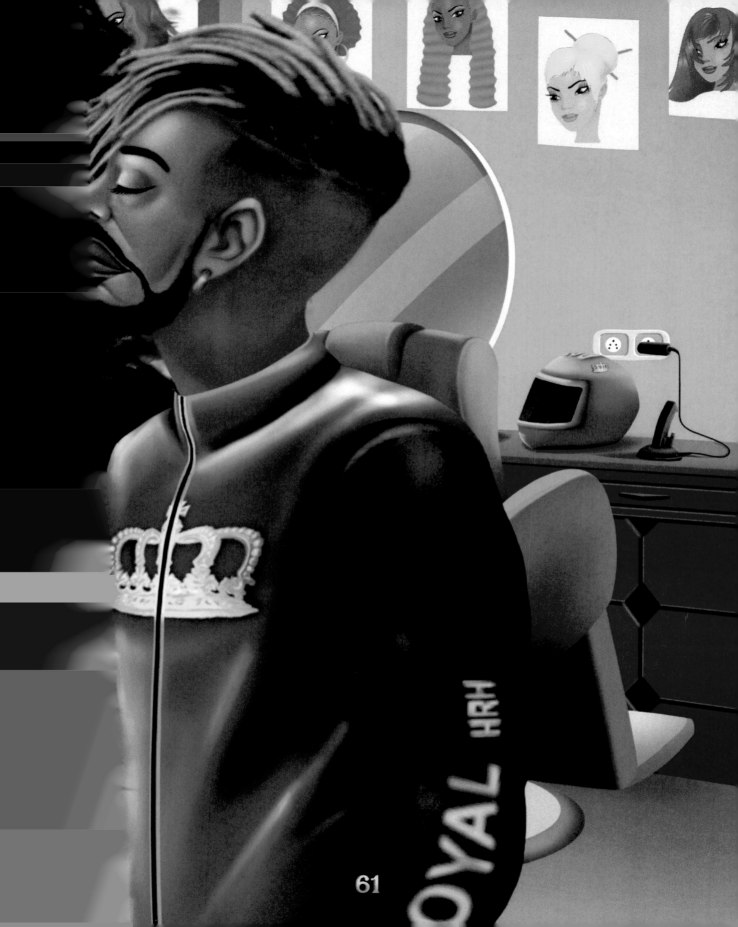

61

The prince kissed 'Rella's wrist
With respect, love and laughter

And took her to be his queen

IN THEIR *Happily* EVER AFTER

The End...

Made in the USA
Columbia, SC
04 September 2022

66412394R00040